DEAR MOUSE FRIENDS, WELCOME TO THE

STONE AGE!

WELCOME TO THE STONE AGE . . . AND THE WORLD OF THE CAVEMICE!

CAPITAL: OLD MOUSE CITY

POPULATION: WE'RE NOT SURE. (MATH DOESN'T EXIST YET!) BUT BESIDES CAVEMICE, THERE ARE PLENTY OF DINOSAURS, <u>WAY</u> TOO MANY SABER-TOOTHED TIGERS, AND FEROCIOUS CAVE BEARS — BUT NO MOUSE HAS EVER HAD THE COURAGE TO COUNT THEM!

TYPICAL FOOD: PETRIFIED CHEESE SOUP

NATIONAL HOLIDAY: GREAT ZAP DAY, WHICH CELEBRATES THE DISCOVERY OF FIRE. RODENTS EXCHANGE GRILLED CHEESE SANDWICHES ON THIS HOLIDAY.

NATIONAL DRINK: MAMMOTH MILKSHAKES

CLIMATE: Unpredictable, WITH FREQUENT METEOR SHOWERS

cheese soup

milkshake

MONEY

SEASHELLS OF ALL SHAPES AND SIZES

MEASUREMENT

THE BASIC UNIT OF MEASUREMENT IS BASED ON THE LENGTH OF THE TAIL OF THE LEADER OF THE VILLAGE. A UNIT CAN BE DIVIDED INTO A HALF TAIL OR QUARTER TAIL. THE LEADER IS ALWAYS READY TO PRESENT HIS TAIL WHEN THERE IS A DISPUTE.

THE CAVEMICE

Geronimo

Trap

Thea

Benjamin

Bugsy Wugsy

Hercule Poirat

Grandma Ratrock

Geronimo Stilton

CAVEMICE

A MAMMOTH MYSTERY

Scholastic Inc.

Published by Scholastic Inc., *Publishers since 1920*, 557 Broadway, New York, NY 10012. SCHOLASTIC and associated logos are trademarks and/or registered trademarks of Scholastic Inc.

Stilton is the name of a famous English cheese. It is a registered trademark of the Stilton Cheese Makers' Association. For more information, go to www.stiltoncheese.com.

ISBN 978-1-338-15917-2

Text by Geronimo Stilton
Original title *Ahi ahi Stiltonùt, è finito il latte di mammut!*
Cover by Flavio Ferron
Illustrations by Giuseppe Facciotto (pencils), Livio Carolina (ink), and Daniele Verzini (color)
Graphics by Marta Lorini

Special thanks to Shannon Decker
Translated by Julia Heim
Interior design by Becky James

10 9 8 7 6 5 4 3 2 1   17 18 19 20 21

Printed in the U.S.A.   40
First printing 2017

MANY AGES AGO, ON PREHISTORIC MOUSE ISLAND, THERE WAS A VILLAGE CALLED OLD MOUSE CITY. IT WAS INHABITED BY BRAVE *RODENT SAPIENS* KNOWN AS THE CAVEMICE.

DANGERS SURROUNDED THE MICE AT EVERY TURN: EARTHQUAKES, METEOR SHOWERS, FEROCIOUS DINOSAURS, AND FIERCE GANGS OF SABER-TOOTHED TIGERS. BUT THE BRAVE CAVEMICE FACED IT ALL WITH A SENSE OF HUMOR, AND WERE ALWAYS READY TO LEND A HAND TO OTHERS.

HOW DO I KNOW THIS? I DISCOVERED AN ANCIENT BOOK WRITTEN BY MY ANCESTOR, GERONIMO STILTONOOT! HE CARVED HIS STORIES INTO STONE TABLETS AND ILLUSTRATED THEM WITH HIS ETCHINGS.

I AM PROUD TO SHARE THESE STONE AGE STORIES WITH YOU. THE EXCITING ADVENTURES OF THE CAVEMICE WILL MAKE YOUR FUR STAND ON END, AND THE JOKES WILL TICKLE YOUR WHISKERS! HAPPY READING!

Geronimo Stilton

WARNING! DON'T IMITATE THE CAVEMICE. WE'RE NOT IN THE STONE AGE ANYMORE!

RUMBLE, RUMBLE, RUMBLE . . .

It was a fabumouse morning in late summer. The sun had just come up, a light **breeze** blew from the sea, and the baby pterodactyls chirped happily. *Ahh* — it was a perfect morning to do some very important work!

My name is Stiltonoot, Geronimo Stiltonoot. I always have very important work to do because I run *The Stone Gazette*, the most FAMOUSE newspaper in all of prehistory! (So what if it's the ONLY one?)

Anyway, that morning I woke up early and climbed behind the wheel of an autosaurus.* I was ready to get my paws in gear!

My sister, Thea, and my associate Wiley Upsnoot were waiting for me impatiently at the entrance to *The Stone Gazette*'s office.

"Boss, you asked us to be ready, and we are!" Upsnoot squeaked. "But, um . . . what are we ready FOR?"

"Inquiring mice need to know!" Thea

* Autosauruses are dinosaurs that transport objects and passengers.

CAWWW!
CAWWW!

continued. "Why in the name of cheese did you, the *laziest* rodent in all of prehistory, wake up so early? And what are you doing on that autosaurus?"

I held up my paws to calm them down. "I called you for **THREE** very simple reasons. **ONE:** the summer heat is already behind us. **TWO:** there's still time before the rainy season. **THREE:** *The Stone Gazette*

Make sense?

is more popular than ever! Make sense?"

"Uh, Boss?" Upsnoot said, tugging on his tail. "I didn't understand a single **coconut** of what you just said . . ."

"Holey boulders, I left out the most **important** thing!" I squeaked. "I asked you to meet me at this unmousely hour because we have no more slabs on which to etch *The Stone Gazette*."

"**What?**" Thea cried. "But how will I write my articles?"

Upsnoot launched into a Paleozoic panic. "And how will I publish my famouse, informative, thirty-slab supplements like 'How to Pick Your Autosaurus'?"

"Well, that's why I called you," I said. "I need your help getting some extra stone slabs from the cavern. This is the pawfect time to do it!"

5

Without a second to waste, we rode the autosaurus up the plateau above Old Mouse City. When we reached the cavern, we got to work. Extracting slabs from the rock is a mousetastically **exhausting** job!

Even so, we worked all morning . . . until Upsnoot accidentally dropped a slab right on my paw.

"**OWWWWW!** What megalithic pain!" I hollered so loudly that it started a landslide from the top of the plateau!

RUMBLE RUMBLE RUMBLE...

the rocks were rolling right toward us. We were going to be MINCED MICE!

Unbelievably, the avalanche stopped just two millitails from us.

PHEW . . . we were saved by a whisker!

STORM COMING!

When the big cloud of DUST caused by the landslide finally vanished, we found a truly mouserific surprise right in front of our snouts: The rolling boulder had cracked other stones, carving out perfectly flat slabs for our prehistoric newspaper!

Triple triceratops horns, it was our LUCKY day!

I scurried over to take a look at the slabs, but slipped on a rock and BANGED snout-first into the slab that Thea and Upsnoot were lifting.

BONK!

The slab split
in two, and a
bump as big
as a coconut
POPPED UP
on my head.
Fossilized feta,
what a day!

"Are you **okay**, little brother?" Thea asked.

"Maybe you should let us take it from here, Boss," Upsnoot suggested.

My head was still **spinning**, so I nodded and stepped off to the side. I grabbed the Jurassic first aid kit and BANDAGED my paw, while Thea and Upsnoot finished loading the slabs. Then Thea lifted me onto the autosaurus, climbed on herself, grabbed the reins, and headed for Old Mouse City.

After riding for a while, Upsnoot suddenly squeaked, "The sky is getting darker . . . a **storm's coming**!"

Fur and fossils — had the rainy season come *early*?

Storm's coming, boss!

"Stay calm," Thea said. "We'll be back in Old Mouse City before a single drop of rain falls!"

But just then . . .

A megalithically loud clap of thunder made us jump out of our fur.

"I don't like the sound of that!" Upsnoot cried.

"Look over there!" Thea squeaked, pointing.

As I followed her paw, I could see a herd of MaMMOtHS racing across the clearing around Old Mouse City. They galloped wildly, making the ground tremble as their fur swung in the wind.

Fossilized fossils, the mammoths seemed super-scared — they were shaken up, frazzled, and totally

terrified!

Mammoths are peaceful animals. They would never hurt anyone. The worst thing they might do is get a bit stinky sometimes . . . but they're scared out of their fur of lightning!

Thea said firmly, "We need to get back to the city before the storm reaches us!"

But at that moment, a gust of wind made the autosaurus swerve. He ended up smashing into the trunk of a Paleozoic palm tree.

BANG!!!

You won't believe it, dear rodent friends, but we had **HIT** the only tree within hundreds of tails!

What megalithic **BaD LUCK**!

CRASH . . .
BAM . . . SPLAT!

Thea didn't get discouraged. She put her snout down and continued steering the autosaurus through the **storm**.

My sister must be the most **DETERMINED** rodent in all of prehistory!

"Come on, big guy!" Thea urged him. "We're almost there!"

Unfortunately, even though the autosaurus's head was as hard as granite, he was still stunned from slamming into the tree. Holey boulders, he was super-**stumbly**!

When we'd almost reached the bottom of the hill, the poor autosaurus accidentally stepped into a hole. He tipped to one side — **WHOAAAAA**!

All the stone slabs fell to the ground, breaking into a thousand tiny pieces.

CRASH!

But that wasn't all . . .

Upsnoot and I were *catapulted* forward! We both fell onto the path with our paws in the air.

BAM!

Good-bye, cavemouse wooooorld!

But since the path headed downhill, we didn't stop there. No, we began to roll in a big heap of snouts and paws, forming a megalithic landslide.

"Good-bye, cavemouse wooooorld!" I squeaked.

"I'm too young to become extinct!" Upsnoot cried.

We tumbled farther and farther until we were more MIXED UP than mammoth milkshakes! Finally, we smacked right into the wall surrounding Old Mouse City.

SPLAT!

Ow, Ow, Ow!

My paws felt like mush, my back was bruised, and my tail was tangled. Basically, I was MINCED MOUSE!

"UGH, I'm not feeling so great, Boss,"

Upsnoot mumbled, massaging his snout.

I nodded, and my head spun. "I was doing a lot better before, too."

Thea and the autosaurus appeared above us. My sister shook her head. "Oh, for all the cheese in Old Mouse City! Are you two okay?"

"I think so." We nodded.

"Good," Thea replied. "We should get going. We need to get back to the city in *two shakes of a mouse's tail*."

We finally made it back to Old Mouse City soaked, bruised, and without a single stone slab for the newspaper. What a megalithic DISASTER!

If all of that was **BAD**, the fleeing of the mammoths was even **worse**.

"What will we do without our mammoth milk?" Thea asked, tugging on her whiskers.

Did you know that mammoth milk is the most **essential** ingredient in mammoth milkshakes, the favorite drink of the cavemice? We had mammoth milkshakes in reserve in case of **EMERGENCY** ... but they wouldn't last long!

Great rocky boulders, we had to do something — and *FAST*!

MAMMOTH MILKSHAKES ARE PREPARED WITH CURDLED MAMMOTH MILK, LEMON JUICE, A PINCH OF SALT, AND WATER.

NO MAMMOTHS, NO MAMMOTH MILKSHAKES!

I hadn't even set paw in my cave when the storm finally hit. There was **LIGHTNING**, **THUNDER**, and *hail* as big as Paleozoic walnuts! In no time, the city was *submerged* in water and mud.

Old Mouse City ground to a halt — no one could go to the market, take a run along the river, or bring the baby autosauruses out for a walk. It was a megalithic **MESS**!

Gasp!

The storm lasted all night. When it finally stopped the next morning, it seemed like an entire **STONE AGE** had passed!

I was about to scamper over to the newsroom, when a shriekodactyl (a shrieking pterodactyl, of course) began YELLING news across the city.

"Listen up, citizens of Old Mouse City!" he announced. "By order of the village leader, Ernest Heftymouse, you are asked to attend a special assembly at the Mammoth Milkshake Pantry — **right now**!"

Listen up!

Triple triceratops' horns! If Ernest Heftymouse was calling an assembly, the mammoth situation must be even **worse** than I'd thought.

23

I left my house as **FAST** as my paws would take me!

The Mammoth Milkshake Pantry was a big cave under the plateau that overlooks Old Mouse City. Inside, **enoRMºUSE** stone containers hold the mammoth milkshake reserves. The drink is so *tasty* and **HYDRATING** that it's one of the cavemice's prized possessions!

The pantry was packed with a crowd of wildly worried rodents.

Ernest Heftymouse stepped to the front of the room. "Dear citizens, I'm afraid I have some megalithically **BAD** news."

So many cavemice!

Our eyes opened wide and we all **held our breaths**. It was quiet enough to hear a whisker twitch.

"Last night's storm caused some very *serious* damage to the mammoth milkshake reserves," Ernest continued.

"**NO!**" we all squeaked at once.

"Water and mud seeped into the stone containers, and the mammoth milkshakes have turned into sticky, stinky, undrinkable sludge!"

"NO!"

"Needless to squeak . . . our reserves are completely ruined."

"NO!"

The mammoth milkshake reserves are ruined!

I couldn't believe my ears!

"So what now?" one rodent asked in despair.

"Let's go to the mammoths!" another suggested. "We can ask for more milk!"

Ernest frowned. "Speaking of the

mammoths . . . during the storm, our pachyderm friends RAN AWAY!"

The crowd was in a full-fledged Paleozoic panic!

"We need an emergency plan!" healer Bluster Conjurat exclaimed. "I propose that we split into TEAMS. Each team can look for the mammoths on a different part of the island."

Massive meteorites, Bluster was right! We needed to find the mammoths and bring them home. It was the only way to get more of our beloved mammoth milkshakes!

We need an emergency plan!

BLUSTER CONJURAT

I already knew what to do: I would team up with Thea, my cousin Trap, and my friend Hercule Poirat, the best detective in all of prehistory.

Ernest Heftymouse assigned us to look for the mammoths around the **Cheddar Volcano**. Bones and stones — that was the most **DANGEROUS** volcano in the cavemouse world!

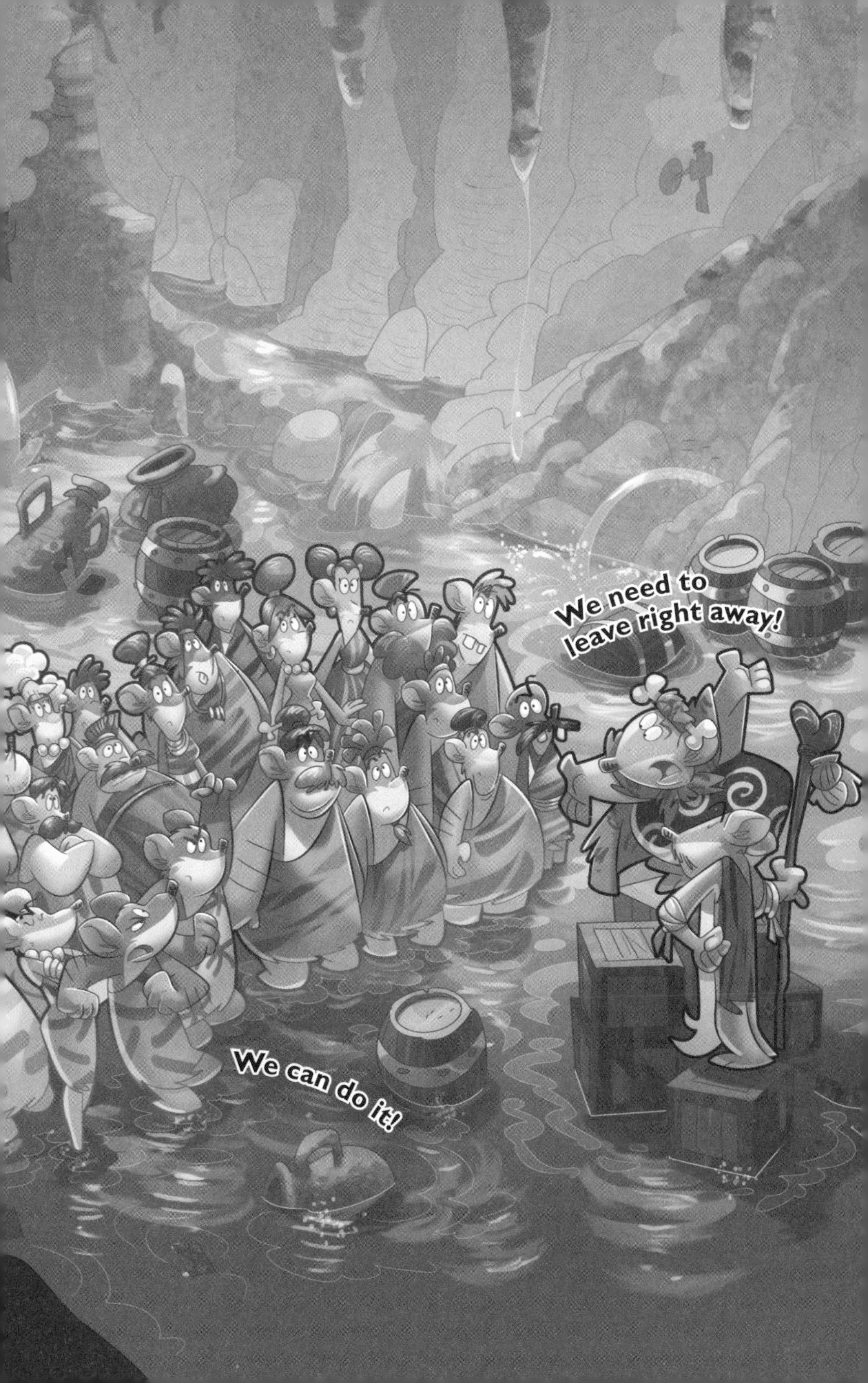
We need to leave right away!
We can do it!

IT'S RAINING . . . HUSKS!

Our team was excited and energized, like mice on a cheese hunt. We needed to find our mammoth friends, and we needed to do it *FAST*!

Squish! Slush! Splash!

But with every step, our paws sunk into the mud left over from the storm. Petrified provolone, it was like walking through a SWAMP!

After what seemed like a whole GEOLOGICAL ERA, we arrived at the foot of the Cheddar Volcano. We ducked into the chestnut forest to rest our aching paws.

"Puff . . . pant . . . huff . . . I can't go any farther!" I collapsed, leaning on the trunk of a tree.

"You're softer than Jurassic mozzarella, Geronimo!" Hercule teased me, nibbling on a banana.

Before I could respond —

BONK!

Something hit me square on the snout.

"**Ow!** What was that?" I squeaked.

I looked up toward the tree branches just in time to see a storm of big, thorny

You're softer than Jurassic mozzarella!

chestnut husks raining down on us!

POCK POCK POCK POCK POCK!

But who . . . what . . . where?!

"Oh no — the **flying squirrels**!" Thea exclaimed, covering her head with her paws.

FLYING SQUIRRELS

CLASSIFICATION: RODENTS OF THE SNEER SNEER SPECIES

HABITAT: CHESTNUT WOODS

CHARACTERISTICS: SPEED, AGILITY, AND GREAT AIM. THEY FLY FROM ONE BRANCH TO ANOTHER, NIBBLING ON PALEOZOIC CHESTNUTS AND PLAYING PRANKS ON ANYONE WHO CROSSES THEIR PATH. THEY CAN BE GROUCHY, SO BE CAREFUL NOT TO MAKE THEM MAD!

You may not know this, but flying squirrels are the rudest animals in all of prehistory. They spend their time flying from one prehistoric tree to the next, thinking up jokes and pranks to pull on whoever crosses their path. In this case, the unlucky target was . . . US!

"Careful! **Incominnng!**" Trap warned, dodging a chestnut husk.

The squirrels did some incredible leaps from one branch to the next. Holey boulders, it really seemed like they were flying!

But we didn't have time to admire their acrobatics. We had to avoid the hailstorm of husks!

OUCH! AHHH! ACK! WHAT A PALEOZOIC PAIN!

Thea thought fast and came up with a solution. She pointed at the empty trunk of a fallen tree. "Let's HIDE in there!"

We all ducked inside the trunk as quickly as our paws would take us. Whew!

"Great rocky boulders, why do those squirrels have it out for us?" I asked, massaging my aching head.

"What a silly question, Geronimo!" Hercule said. "Those nice little animals don't have it out for us — they're just defending their territory."

"Nice little animals?" I cried. "They turned me into a Paleozoic pincushion!"

"Come on, Cousin," Trap said, rolling his eyes. "How about instead of complaining, you think of a way to get us out of here? Aren't you the brains of the family?"

"Yeah!" Hercule squeaked, elbowing me. "What's your genius idea?"

Bones and stones, what was I supposed to say now?

SHRIEEEEEK!
SHRIEEEEEK!

I didn't have a single coconut of an idea what to do next!

SHRIEEEEK!
SHRIEEEEEK!

A sudden sharp, piercing sound made us all jump out of our fur.

"What was that noise?" I yelped.

"**Quiet**, you Jurassic fool!" Hercule said. "You mean to tell me you don't recognize it?"

Had I **lost my cheese**? What was Hercule squeaking about? "Should I be worried?" I mumbled.

"Of course you should!" Thea said. "That's the call of one of the most **DANGEROUS** and cunning predators of the Stone Age!"

Boulders of Brie, just what we needed! My whiskers began wobbling in fright.

"It's a **Fiery Falcon**," my sister continued, "the flying squirrels' number one enemy! And it must be **VERRRRY** hungry, based on how loudly it's shrieking . . ."

Sure enough, hearing the falcon's distinct cry, the squirrels *darted off* to hide in

Fiery Falcon

CLASSIFICATION: A PREDATOR OF THE FANGOOT FALCONOOT FAMILY

HABITAT: ANYWHERE THERE'S FOOD!

CHARACTERISTICS: FALCON FACE, FALCON BEAK, FALCON TALONS, FALCON FEATHERS . . . BUT AS HUNGRY AS A WOLF!

the tree branches. That falcon was definitely looking for a snack!

We stayed still and quiet in our hiding place. After what seemed like a geological era, I felt an annoying tingling in my paw. Petrified provolone, I really needed to sit down!

I changed positions and — SQUeak!

I had accidentally sat right on top of a chestnut husk!

I leaped up and POPPED right through the hollow tree trunk with my head. OUCH, what megalithic pain! But even worse . . . GULP!

Now I was face-to-face with the Fiery Falcon!

I let out a prehistoric SQUeak — a mixture of pain and terror. This was it! I was

really extinct now!
Squeak!

My squeak was so loud that I actually scared the falcon — and he **flew away**! Jurassic Jack cheese, I couldn't believe it!

But then I fell, as heavy as a boulder, and landed on my poor undertail again.

BONK!

Oh, for all the thorns on a cactus! I was sore all over and shaking from the ends of my

1. I burst through the top of the hollow trunk . . .

2. Came face-to-face with the falcon . . .

3. And landed smack on my undertail! Youch!

whiskers to the tip of my tail — but I was safe. **Whew!**

Thea, Trap, and Hercule rushed out of their hiding place in the empty trunk.

"**FABUMOUSE** job, little brother!" Thea cheered.

"Taking off like that was a **marvemouse**

Fabumouse job, Geronimo!

Umm . . .

idea," Trap agreed, looking shocked. "How did you do that?"

"Umm, well . . . I've been exercising . . ." I stammered, rubbing my sore tail.

"SEE?" Hercule said, putting a paw around my shoulders. "You've learned a thing or two from spending so much time with me!"

"Well, actually —" I said.

"Quick!" Thea interrupted. "Let's get our tails in gear before the flying squirrels come out of HIDING."

Together, we left the woods as fast as our paws would take us. We had to find those MISSING MAMMOTHS!

YUCK!

We crossed a large, flat area. Unfortunately, the rain had made the ground really sticky, really muddy, and really squishy.

YUCK!

Walking was megalithically *exhausting*! Plus, we didn't spot a single trace of the mammoths.

Just when I thought things couldn't possibly get worse, we found ourselves facing a stretch of quicksand!

Hercule put up a paw. "**STOP** and hush! Something's not right . . ."

"You're telling me," I said. "I'm not going

through that **quicksand**!"

"No, Geronimo, that's not what I mean! Don't you smell that horrific $TENCH?"

Hercule is the best detective in all of prehistory (plus, he's the only one!) and he almost **NEVER** makes a mistake.

"Let's see . . . how **strange**!" he went on, sniffing the air with a concerned expression on his snout. "I can't figure out what type of stench it is."

Dinosaur droppings?

Rotten bananas?

Umm . . .

Is it Trap's paws?

"I don't smell a thing!" Trap said, sniffing with his snout in the air.

"I believe that," I said. "You haven't taken a bath in at least FIVE geological eras! You have such a strong stench, you can't smell anything else . . ."

"Hey, I just bathed two months ago!" Trap protested.

Hercule suddenly squeaked and clapped his paws over our mouths. "HUSH! I figured it out — I smell the stench of the SABER-TOOTHED TIGERS!"

HEE, HEE, HEE!

Holey rolling boulders! Saber-toothed tigers? The ENEMIES of us cavemice? The sharp-fanged

44

clan of Tiger Khan? We were in enormouse trouble!

We couldn't go back, because we would end up in Tiger Khan's **clutches**. But we couldn't go forward, either, because the path was covered with **quicksand**.

We were trapped! Doomed! Extinct! Mousemeat!

I was about to etch out my last will and

Follow me!

testament, when Hercule led us into a grove of reeds. He grabbed a hollow reed and said seriously, "Follow me!"

Hercule darted out from behind the reeds and jumped into an enormouse **MUDDY** pond next to the path.

SPLOOSH!

A moment later, Hercule's reed popped out of the mud.

Bones and stones, **NOW** I understood! We would hide in that **super-stinky** muddy pond, using the hollow reeds as snorkels for breathing.

"Fabumouse idea!" Thea cried.

A moment later, she and Trap each grabbed a reed and **LEAPED** into the mud and muck. Petrified provolone, what choice did I have but to follow them? With a reed in my paw, I stepped up to the edge of the horrifyingly **MUDDY** swamp.

Fossilized feta, what a **horrible** stench!

Before heading in, I noticed something big and round floating nearby.

"Guys, I found a . . . a . . ."

I had no idea what I had found!

"Well, I found something that we can hold on to while we're in the mud!"

Hercule stuck his snout up out of the

mud. "Wow, Geronimo, you're right! That will work perfectly — we can grab on to this so that we don't get pulled away by the current."

On Hercule's signal, all four of us held on and ducked under the mud. We stayed **pawsitively still** as four saber-toothed tigers passed by.

I was as **PETRIFIED** as an ancient fossil!

Thankfully, the nasty cats didn't notice anything unusual and disappeared out of sight.

"**PheW!**" I squeaked, popping up out of the mud. "That was close!"

"Yeah, but where were those fanged felines headed?" Thea asked.

Trap shrugged. "Hopefully *FAR, FAR AWAY* from here!"

Once the coast was clear, we climbed out

of the mud puddle, dragging that **strange** megalithic floating mass behind us.

Hercule pulled out his magnifying glass to take a closer look at it.

"Holey boulders — this is a **fossilized dinosaur dropping**!" he squeaked.

Thea, Trap, and I looked at one another with horrified expressions on our snouts. While we were submerged in that stinky mud, we'd been holding on to . . .

DINOSAUR POO?

How prehistorically **gross**!

A TERRIBLE SURPRISE!

We continued our search, but we didn't spot even the **shadow** of a mammoth!

With our tails between our legs, we decided to turn back. Unfortunately, a truly TERRIBLE surprise awaited us in Old Mouse City . . .

The fence that protected the city was surrounded by fierce saber-toothed tigers, led by Tiger Khan himself.

I clapped my paws over my eyes. "Petrified provolone, we're FINISHED!" I squeaked.

This was where the nasty cats we'd hidden from had been heading! They wanted to turn the citizens of Old Mouse City into rodent kabobs! And without our mammoth friends to defend us, we were in a megalithic **ton** of trouble.

We spied on the tigers from a safe distance. "Now what?" I whispered.

I couldn't help the Paleozoic panic rising inside me. My beloved nephew Benjamin was inside the village. I had to **protect** him!

Thea looked more determined than ever. "Never give up. We'll figure something out!"

Never give up!

Meanwhile, the tigers were building wooden ladders that they could use to **scale** the wall.

Just then Hercule pointed a paw. **"LOOK!"**

Giant glaciers, two of the tigers had captured a . . . **MaMMoth CuB**!

The poor little — well, **BiG**! — guy! He must have gotten lost when the rest of the mammoth herd fled. The tigers had found him, captured him, and tied him up like Jurassic string cheese.

"**Squeak!** I wouldn't want to be in his

place," Trap whispered. "Surely those terrible tigers will take him to their encampment in the Stinky Swamp!"

"Those nasty cats could use a good club to the head," Thea said, frowning.

"You want to FIGHT the tigers?" I asked, whiskers wobbling. "B-b-but what if they CAPTURE us?"

Squeak!

55

Thea grinned. "**Don't worry** — I've got a solution!"

Hercule and I looked at her hopefully.

"We need to find the mammoths!" Thea said matter-of-factly.

"Crusty cheese chunks, thanks a lot!" Hercule said. "Do you think we're a bunch of **cheesebrains**?"

"We already tried to look for the mammoths, remember?" I added.

"Listen to me," Thea said calmly. "If the mammoths knew that one of their **babies** had been captured by the tigers, they would come back for him. I bet they'd also teach those **nasty cats** a lesson!"

Rocky boulders, maybe my sister was right!

"I agree," said Hercule. "But there's still one **enormouse** problem — how will we track down the mammoths in the first place?"

"Maybe we could send one of our **MAIL-A-DACTYLS*** out to deliver a message to the mammoths," I suggested.

But Hercule shook his snout. "The mammoths don't know how to **read**! We can't send them a written message."

Trap looked thoughtful. "What if we tried **smoke signals**?"

"Megalithic mozzarella!" Hercule cried, exasperated. "Everyone knows that the mammoths have **TERRIBLE EYESIGHT**. Plus, do any of you know smoke signals?"

"Um, well, no . . . " I said with a shrug. "But then what can we do?"

My question hung in the air while we all stared at Hercule.

After a moment, he cleared his throat and

* Mail-a-dactyls are flying dinosaurs that deliver messages etched on giant stone slabs.

57

a clever smile stretched across his snout. "You're not going to believe your **EARS**, cavemice!"

"Try us," I said, eager to hear Hercule's plan.

He clapped his paws.

"I have the most mouserific idea in all of prehistory!"

"So what are you waiting for?" Thea cried. "Tell us!"

MASSIVE METEORITES, WE JUST MIGHT BE CLOSE TO FINDING AN ANSWER TO OUR ENORMOUSE PROBLEM!

AN IDEA WITH WINGS!

Hercule gave another dramatic pause, then finally exclaimed, "The answer is simple. We will **FLY**!"

Bones and stones — **what**? Trap, Thea, and I looked at one another in confusion.

"But, Hercule, I think you're forgetting one small detail," Thea said slowly. "We don't know **HOW** to fly!"

"Right, we don't have wings," I added. Had Hercule **lost his cheese**?

"You really are a bunch of **GRANITEHEADS**!" Hercule responded, rolling his eyes. "Did I say that we would fly with wings? **HUH?**"

"Well, no . . ." Trap said.

"That's right!" Hercule went on. "My dear friends, we will fly — on a **Balloonosaurus**!"

Thea, Trap, and I all jumped to our paws. Fossilized feta, that really was a **MEGALITHIC IDEA**!

Balloonosauruses are flying **DINOSAURS** that we cavemice use for long air trips. They have wings, and for gas they use a normal, seasoned, or spicy **bean fuel**! Their runway is at the Old Mouse City flightport.

I paced on my paws, thinking hard. "But . . . to get to the flightport, we need to cross the

Burp!

city. How will we avoid the TIGERS camped out around the city wall?"

"I have a PLAN!" Thea said. "Listen up . . ."

1 First, we will enter Old Mouse City at nighttime, sneaking through the secret entrance in the dark so we won't be discovered.

2 Then, as quiet as mice, we will scurry to the flightport to board a balloonosaurus.

3 Finally, we will survey the island from ABOVE in search of the mammoths.

It was a brilliant and DANGEROUS plan. Oh, who am I kidding? It was so dangerous that we were risking extinction!

"Pointy triceratops horns, those tigers will spot us!" I squeaked in a panic. "They'll capture us! They'll pulverize us!"

"Do you have a better idea?" Thea asked.

"We have to do something, and this might work."

As much as I hated to admit it, Thea was right. The future of all cavemice was at stake!

So, in the DEAD OF NiGHT, we crept up to the city wall and silently crawled through the mud. We were only two millitails away from TIGER KHAN and his fanged henchmen!

1 TAKE ADVANTAGE OF THE DARK . . .

2 FIND A BALLOONOSAURUS

3 SURVEY THE ISLAND FROM ABOVE, LOOKING FOR MAMMOTHS!

Zzzz!
Zzzz!

Luckily, the fearsome felines were busy dreaming up the different ways they could cook us cavemice.

"Stewed, roasted, or baked?" one asked, licking his lips.

"No, rodent kabobs!"

"As a side, would potatoes or Paleozoic onions be better?"

"Onions! And it's even better if they're MOLDY — extra flavor! Ha, ha, ha!"

Before I could stop myself, I let out a grunt of disgust.

"UGH!"

Tiger Khan perked up his ears and SCANNED the dark with his ferocious eyes. Squeeeeeak, what had I done?

Luckily, Hercule and Trap had a plan to save our tails. They began to make similar noises.

"UGGGGH! HOO–HOO–HOOOO!"

"Oh, it's just a Jurassic owl," Tiger Khan growled, disappointed. He'd fallen for our trick!

Boulders of Brie, we had almost been GONERS!

Without a second to waste, we used the secret entrance in the wall to Old Mouse

City. It was made for **EMERGENCIES** — and this definitely qualified!

When we reached the flightport, we found the balloonosauruses snoring happily. Holey boulders, they were sleeping as heavily as blocks of **GRANITE**!

We managed to wake one up, but he had two shriveled wings and a goofy expression on his face. We couldn't afford to be picky, though — we had to get going!

We climbed aboard the balloonosaurus and took off just as a lightning bolt lit up the sky.

ZAP!

Jurassic Jack cheese! Just what we needed — another storm!

ZAP!

The balloonosaurus had just taken off, and I was already as GREEN as a Jurassic zucchini from fear, vertigo, and airsickness. I was a mousetastic MESS!

"Be brave, Geronimo!" Trap hollered, giving me a thump on the back.

"OUCH!" I yelped. What Paleozoic pain!

Suddenly, a gust of WIND made the basket of the balloonosaurus toss from one side to the other. I tumbled to the bottom of

Gulp!

the basket with my paws
in the air.

BONK!

But that was just
the beginning. The
wind began to
blow harder
and harder
until . . .

BOOM!

Thunder ECHOED

all around us. This was going to be a
megalithic storm!

Our goofy balloonosaurus had trouble
keeping his balance when the sky was calm.
In the middle of a storm, forget it!
The poor guy wheezed and panted, flapping
his shriveled wings and weaving every

Helllllp!

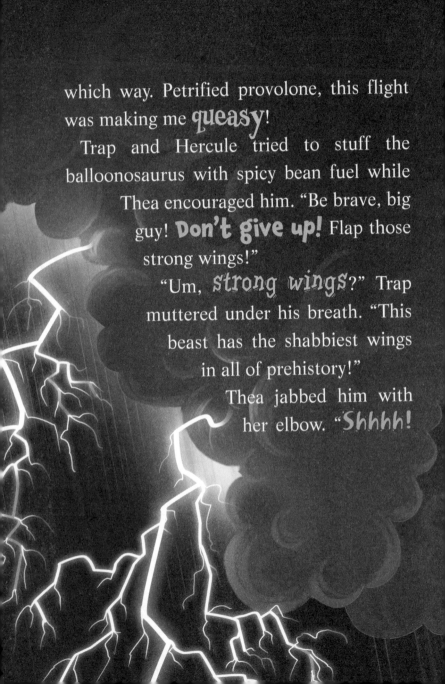

which way. Petrified provolone, this flight was making me **queasy**!

Trap and Hercule tried to stuff the balloonosaurus with spicy bean fuel while Thea encouraged him. "Be brave, big guy! **Don't give up!** Flap those strong wings!"

"Um, *strong wings*?" Trap muttered under his breath. "This beast has the shabbiest wings in all of prehistory!"

Thea jabbed him with her elbow. "**Shhhh!**

Can't you see that he's doing his best?

Just then a **super-powerful** lightning bolt ripped through the clouds and struck the balloonosaurus's tail. The poor dinosaur swerved dangerously and began to spiral down out of the sky. Holey boulders, we were all **doomed**!

"**NOOOOO!**" Thea yelled. "Don't give up now! You can do it! Take us higher! Come on, come on, come on!"

But despite her encouragement, the balloonosaurus *FELL* like a sack of potatoes — and *WE FELL WITH HIM*!

GREAT GOUDA GLACIERS, WE WERE JUST A PAWSTEP AWAY FROM EXTINCTION!

I did the only thing I could do at that moment: I hugged my friends and prepared for the worst, squeaking at the top of my lungs,

"GOOD-BYE, CAVEMOUSE WORRRRRLD!"

SAVED BY A WHISKER!

We kept falling but never hit the ground! Finally, I opened my eyes, and amazingly, I **wasn't** extinct. Instead, I found myself sitting on something soft and comfortable. I looked up and found myself snout-to-trunk

Snort!

Um …

with — squeak! — a mammoth!

I had landed right on his trunk!

The beast looked annoyed. I had landed right on top of him in the middle of the night — with no warning!

"Um, well . . ." I said, giving him my most fabumouse smile. Before he could get any ANGRIER, I jumped down to the muddy ground next to Thea, Trap, and Hercule.

Our balloonosaurus, on the other paw, had landed in a small lake nearby. The poor guy was having a tough time getting out of the water!

"Here, grab on to this!" called Thea, throwing him a rope.

With the last of his strength, the balloonosaurus snagged the rope, dragged himself to shore, and collapsed on the ground.

He looked just about as bad as I felt!

But I couldn't think about that, because the mammoth I had landed on was stomping our way — and he looked **MAD**.

HEEELLLPPPPP!

Thea held up a paw. "**STOP!** We have something to tell you!"

She began to tell him everything that had happened, while Trap and Hercule tried to act out her words so the mammoth would understand.

"The saber-toothed tigers have **ATTACKED** Old Mouse City!"

Trap did a pirouette.

"They **CAPTURED** a baby mammoth!"

Hercule jumped in the air four times, while Trap grimaced.

The mammoth froze in **shock**. Then

he raised himself onto his back legs and let out a loud trumpet:

"BHRUUAAH!"

The ground began to shake. Fossilized feta, what was happening? A moment later, we were surrounded by an entire **HERD** of mammoths!

"BHRUUAAH! BHRUUAAH!"
BHRUUAAH!

They sounded furious!

"They're going to rescue the baby!" Hercule squeaked.

"And I'll bet they teach those terrible tigers a *LESSON*, too!" Trap exclaimed.

"What are we waiting for, guys?" Thea cried, fiercer than ever.

"CHARRRRRRGE!"

The mammoths let us climb on their backs, and the herd raced toward Old Mouse City.

HOORAY!
The mammoths and cavemice were about to get our revenge!

MAMMOTH ATTACK!

The mammoths *RAN* through the night, despite the wind, the dark, and the deep, sticky mud. They were fabumouse!

DRIP! DROP! DRIP!

The rain was coming down heavier and heavier now. **WHAT A STORM!**

I held on to the back of the mammoths' leader for dear life. Holey boulders, I was getting tossed around so much that I felt like a mammoth milkshake myself!

"Don't let go, Geronimo! HOLD ON TIGHT!" Thea called over the storm.

At the first light of dawn, we finally arrived at Old Mouse City.

The saber-toothed tigers had finished building their ladders. They were about to climb the wall and invade the city!

"We're going to have the purrfect

cavemouse **feast**," Tiger Khan snarled.

"Har, har, har!" his henchcats replied.

PETRIFIED PROVOLONE, WE DIDN'T HAVE A MINUTE TO LOSE!

When the mammoths spotted the tigers, they began to trumpet at them.

BHRUUAAH! BHRUUAAH! BHRUUAAH!

"What's going on?" Tiger Khan **SCREECHED**.

The fierce felines on the wooden ladders stopped, confused. But the mammoths didn't even give the saber-toothed tigers time to **defend** themselves.

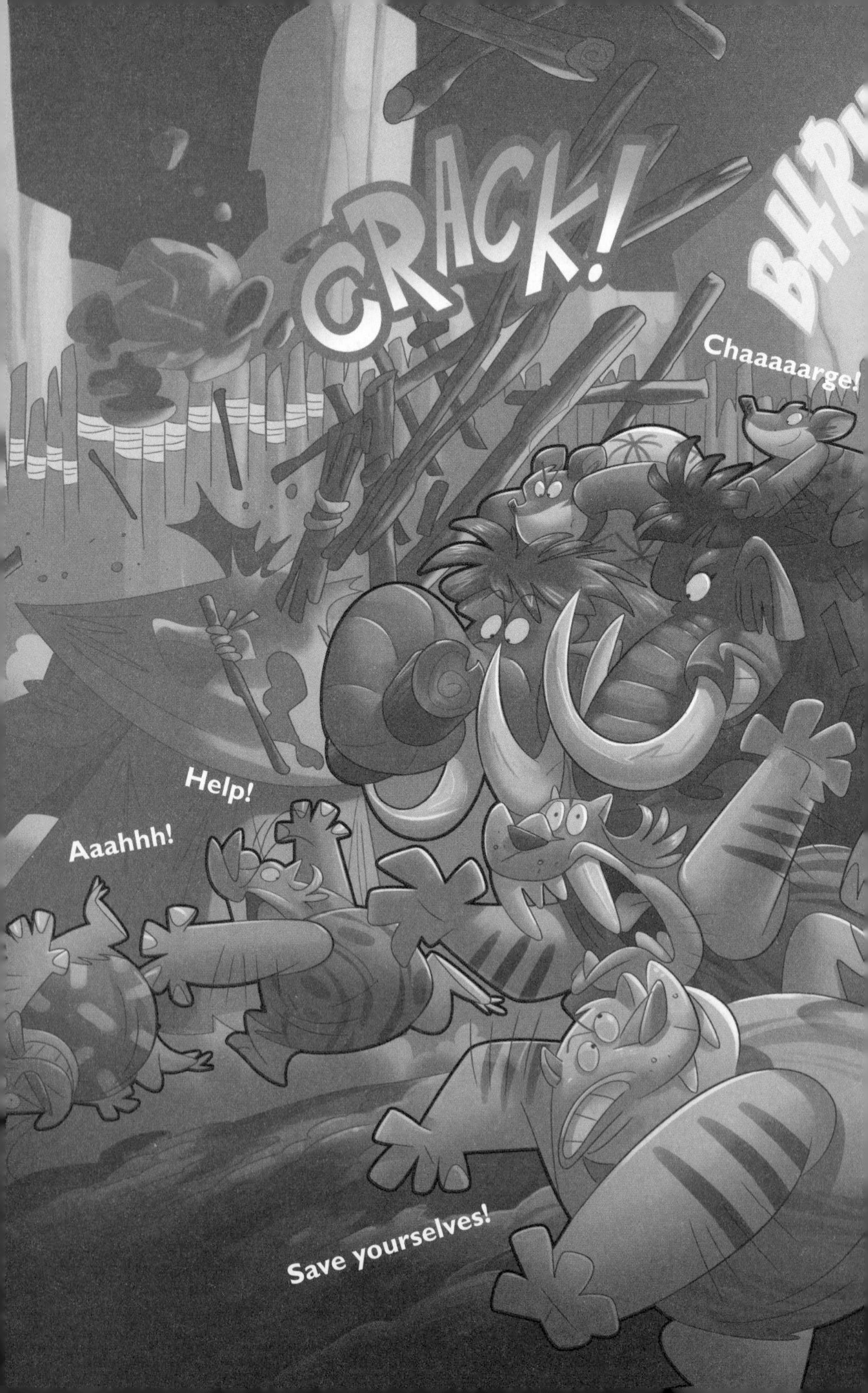
CRACK!
Chaaaaaarge!
Help!
Aaahhh!
Save yourselves!

Great Gouda glaciers, it was an *INCREDIBLE* sight: The mammoths completely petrified Tiger Khan and his henchcats. They wiped out those felines like *PREHISTORIC BOWLING PINS*!

Many of the tigers ended up in the **MUD** with their paws in the air. Others *RAN AWAY* like Jurassic jackrabbits. Others *yelped* like scared little kittens.

"HELP! LET US GO!"

"THAT'S ENOUGH!"

Even the terrible Tiger Khan ran away with his tail between his legs. **Holey boulders!**

On the other paw, the baby mammoth that the tigers had captured was thrilled — he was *FINALLY* back with his herd!

As soon as the tigers were all out of sight, I scampered over and **hugged** the leader of the mammoths as hard as I could. Bones and stones, our mammoth friends were true heroes!

WHAT WOULD WE HAVE DONE WITHOUT THEM?

Thank you, my friend!

I'M PROUD OF YOU, UNCLE GERONIMO!

What a mouserific moment!

And to make it even better, the storm stopped. The sun finally started shining again!

We climbed back onto the mammoths and made our triumphant entrance into the city.

"Hooray! Long live the heroes of Old Mouse City!" We were surrounded by cheering rodents, led by the village leader, Ernest Heftymouse.

Holey boulders, how exciting!

My mammoth signaled for me to climb down. Then he ran to the baby and surrounded him with cuddles.

Wait one WHISKER-LOVING minute! Bones and stones — that mammoth was the little one's **dad**!

What a fabumouse SURPRISE!

I let out a sigh of relief. It was marvemouse to be home again after that long, FUR-RAISING night.

"What a megalithic **triumph**! You saved Old Mouse City, and you brought the mammoths back!" Ernest Heftymouse proclaimed, turning to me and my friends. "Now we can **restock** our mammoth milkshake reserves!"

"**Hooray** for the Stiltonoots! **Hooray** for the mammoths!" all the Old Mouse City rodents squeaked at the tops of their lungs.

To celebrate, they lifted each of us **HIGH** into the air, one by one.

When it was my turn, however, Ernest Heftymouse began to squeak again. "In the name of everyone in Old Mouse City, I want to officially **thank** Geronimo, Thea, Trap, Hercule, and all our mammoth friends!"

The rodents who had tossed me in the air turned to applaud — and **forgot** to catch me!

SPLAT!

I ended up whisker-deep in a giant mud puddle!

Why do things like this always happen to **ME**?

I lifted my snout from the **MUD** and wiped my paws across my eyes.

"You were great, Uncle!" a little voice squeaked just then.

Oof!

HUH?

Massive meteorites, it was my nephew Benjamin!

Even though I was soaking wet and covered in mud, Benjamin leaped into my arms.

"You saved Old Mouse City! I'm so proud of you, Uncle!"

At that moment, I forgot all about the mud and my bumps and bruises. I just melted into Benjamin's hug like Jurassic Brie left out in the sun!

SPRIIITTTZZZ!

After this crazy adventure, the friendship between the mammoths and the cavemice was **stronger** than ever.

Papa mammoth, who had brought me to Old Mouse City, seemed like he wanted to say something.

"BHRUAH . . . BHRUAH . . . BHRUAH, BHRUAH!"

"Did I get that right? You mammoths want to give us a gift?" I asked. "You'll give us a **DOUBLE** ration of curdled milk until we get our reserves back?" I went on translating. "Well, that's . . . rattastic!"

Papa mammoth nodded happily, waving his trunk.

Fossilized feta, in just a few days we could restore our reserves of mammoth milk! What a mousetastic relief!

Papa mammoth smiled. Then, before I knew what was happening, he sucked up a pool of muddy water with his trunk . . . and sprayed it at me!

SPLASSSSSSH!

Gulp!

Overwhelmed by the super-powerful stream of water and mud, I was **knocked off my paws** and splatted on the ground twenty tails away. Holey rolling boulders!

"Wow, Geronimo, I think he **likes** you!" Hercule exclaimed, laughing under his whiskers. "Didn't you know that spraying water is a sign of affection for mammoths?"

"Oh . . . well . . . **THANKS A LOT**!" I responded, wringing out my soaked tail.

A few days later, the mammoths returned to graze on the plateaus near the city.

Thanks to their generosity, our mammoth milk reserves were **full** again!

Ernest Heftymouse called for a day of celebration. "We will thank our heroes with a **lavish banquet** in their honor!"

His wife, Chattina Heftymouse, held up a paw to stop Ernest. "**Quit your squeaking!**

This is just an **excuse** for you to stuff your snout with food!"

Ernest turned **red** in the snout. "But I . . . the banquet . . . the mammoths . . ."

"Not another squeak! Look at that **big belly** of yours," Chattina said. "A village leader who respects himself should be agile,

All you think about is food!

But I . . .

quick, and in good shape. He should set a fabumouse example for his fellow mice!"

It was too bad, because a banquet would have been marvemouse! We were all starting to feel a bit sorry for poor Ernest, too.

"Oh, come on, Chattina," Trap said. "Be reasonable!"

"Jurassic Jarlsberg, we earned a banquet!" Hercule added.

"Plus," Thea said, "a party with everyone all together sounds pretty **fabumouse**, doesn't it?"

"Oh, all right . . ." Chattina conceded. "We'll have the party, but on a few conditions."

Here were Chattina's rules:

1 The party wouldn't be held RIGHT AWAY; we'd have it two days later.

2 During the two days of preparation, Ernest would eat **ONLY** prehistoric salad and Paleozoic fresh fruit.

3 During these two days, Ernest would also have to keep in shape by *RUNNING* around Old Mouse City from dawn until dusk.

4 Thea, Trap, Hercule, and I would run with Ernest to make sure that he didn't **stuff his snout** in secret!

Hercule tried to protest. "But that's not fair! So we **ALSO** have to run and eat only fruit and vegetables?"

"Well, it certainly won't hurt you!" Chattina said. "That's the deal — **take it or leave it.**"

"Don't worry, Chattina," Thea said with a wink. "I'll make sure that they're all training properly!"

So as we waited for the banquet, we began to *RUN* and eat healthy foods under the supervision of our trainer, Thea.

"Come on, **lazypaws**!" my fabumously fit sister squeaked. "Move those legs! A nice run will do you good!"

One, two . . . one, two . . . one, two!

FOSSILIZED FETA, HOW EXHAUSTING!

A SPECIAL REWARD

At the end of two intense days of dieting and training, I was basically **mousemeat**. And I wasn't the only one — Trap, Hercule, and Ernest Heftymouse were all megalithically tired, too!

Thea, on the other paw, was full of energy. "Come on, musclemice! It's time to celebrate!"

After we bathed and changed, we joined our fellow citizens for the banquet.

HOLEY BOULDERS — IT WAS ABOUT TIME!

Just as it was about to begin, we all heard a **STRANGE SOUND** coming from the entrance to the city.

PETRIFIED PARMESAN, WHO COULD IT BE?

Had the **TIGERS** come back?

"Don't get your tails in a twist!" Thea said, peeking through a hole in the city wall. "It's nothing **DANGEROUS**."

We opened the doors to find an exhausted, filthy, shaken, and singed balloonosaurus!

Puff! Pant!

"That's our **BALLOONOSAURUS**!" I exclaimed.

It was the **SAME** balloonosaurus that had brought me, Thea, Trap, and Hercule to search for the mammoths!

The poor dinosaur stepped toward us, but a moment later . . .

THUD!

He collapsed to the ground.

Holey boulders, we had completely forgotten about him! He'd had to return to the city alone. **Poor guy!**

"We have to **help** him!" Thea declared.

"Pawsitively," I said. "Thanks to him, we were able to save Old Mouse City from the saber-toothed tigers!"

"JUST A MINUTE," Trap protested, holding up a paw. "What about the party?"

"Patience, Trap," Thea said with a sigh. "Don't be selfish!"

So before the banquet began, we all put our paws together to give our heroic balloonosaurus a fabumouse scented bath! We **massaged** his tired wings and filled his belly with a special reward: a triple serving of super-spicy **bean fuel**, of course!

Without him, how would we have found the mammoths? How would we have saved Old Mouse City from the clutches of the SABER-TOOTHED TIGERS?

Once we'd properly thanked him, the banquet could **finally** begin!

When we reached the enormouse table, we found Ernest Heftymouse about to sink his teeth into a giant round of Volcanico cheese, the most delicious — and **stinky** — cheese in the prehistoric world.

"Ernest Heftymouse!" Chattina squeaked. "What are you doing?"

The village leader looked at his wife with **BIG**, innocent eyes.

Chattina rolled her own eyes. "You just want to stuff your snout!"

As they continued to argue, Thea, Trap, Hercule, and I sat down at the table and enjoyed all the cavemice specialties — along with bowls and bowls and bowls of mammoth milkshakes!

PALEOZOIC PROVOLONE, WHAT A RATTASTIC PARTY!

And not just because of the great food. The banquet stood for so much more than that!

Old Mouse City had been saved, we had reinforced our historic friendship with the mammoths, and my whole family was there to celebrate with me. What more could

I possibly want? Nothing, dear rodent friends! Everything was pawsitively *perfect* the way it was.

But just in case, I'll always be ready for my next adventure in the Stone Age, or I'm not

Geronimo Stiltonoot, Cavemouse!

Don't miss any of my special edition adventures!

THE KINGDOM OF FANTASY

THE QUEST FOR PARADISE:
THE RETURN TO THE KINGDOM OF FANTASY

THE AMAZING VOYAGE:
THE THIRD ADVENTURE IN THE KINGDOM OF FANTASY

THE DRAGON PROPHECY:
THE FOURTH ADVENTURE IN THE KINGDOM OF FANTASY

THE VOLCANO OF FIRE:
THE FIFTH ADVENTURE IN THE KINGDOM OF FANTASY

THE SEARCH FOR TREASURE:
THE SIXTH ADVENTURE IN THE KINGDOM OF FANTASY

THE ENCHANTED CHARMS:
THE SEVENTH ADVENTURE IN THE KINGDOM OF FANTASY

THE PHOENIX OF DESTINY:
AN EPIC KINGDOM OF FANTASY ADVENTURE

THE HOUR OF MAGIC:
THE EIGHTH ADVENTURE IN THE KINGDOM OF FANTASY

THE WIZARD'S WAND:
THE NINTH ADVENTURE IN THE KINGDOM OF FANTASY

THE SHIP OF SECRETS:
THE TENTH ADVENTURE IN THE KINGDOM OF FANTASY

THE DRAGON OF FORTUNE:
AN EPIC KINGDOM OF FANTASY ADVENTURE

THE JOURNEY THROUGH TIME

BACK IN TIME:
THE SECOND JOURNEY THROUGH TIME

THE RACE AGAINST TIME:
THE THIRD JOURNEY THROUGH TIME

LOST IN TIME:
THE FOURTH JOURNEY THROUGH TIME

Be sure to read all my fabumouse adventures!

#1 Lost Treasure of the Emerald Eye

#2 The Curse of the Cheese Pyramid

#3 Cat and Mouse in a Haunted House

#4 I'm Too Fond of My Fur!

#5 Four Mice Deep in the Jungle

#6 Paws Off, Cheddarface!

#7 Red Pizzas for a Blue Count

#8 Attack of the Bandit Cats

#9 A Fabumouse Vacation for Geronimo

#10 All Because of a Cup of Coffee

#11 It's Halloween, You 'Fraidy Mouse!

#12 Merry Christmas, Geronimo!

#13 The Phantom of the Subway

#14 The Temple of the Ruby of Fire

#15 The Mona Mousa Code

#16 A Cheese-Colored Camper

#17 Watch Your Whiskers, Stilton!

#18 Shipwreck on the Pirate Islands

#19 My Name Is Stilton, Geronimo Stilton

#20 Surf's Up, Geronimo!

#21 The Wild, Wild West

#22 The Secret of Cacklefur Castle

A Christmas Tale

#23 Valentine's Day Disaster

#24 Field Trip to Niagara Falls

#25 The Search for Sunken Treasure

#26 The Mummy with No Name

#27 The Christmas Toy Factory

#28 Wedding Crasher

#29 Down and Out Down Under

#30 The Mouse Island Marathon

#31 The Mysterious Cheese Thief

Christmas Catastrophe

#32 Valley of the Giant Skeletons

#33 Geronimo and the Gold Medal Mystery

#34 Geronimo Stilton, Secret Agent

#35 A Very Merry Christmas

#36 Geronimo's Valentine

#37 The Race Across America

#38 A Fabumouse School Adventure

#39 Singing Sensation

#40 The Karate Mouse

#41 Mighty Mount Kilimanjaro

#42 The Peculiar Pumpkin Thief

#43 I'm Not a Supermouse!

#44 The Giant Diamond Robbery

#45 Save the White Whale!

#46 The Haunted Castle

#47 Run for the Hills, Geronimo!

#48 The Mystery in Venice

#49 The Way of the Samurai

#50 This Hotel Is Haunted!

#51 The Enormouse Pearl Heist

#52 Mouse in Space!

#53 Rumble in the Jungle

#54 Get into Gear, Stilton!

#55 The Golden Statue Plot

#56 Flight of the Red Bandit

The Hunt for the Golden Book

#57 The Stinky Cheese Vacation

#58 The Super Chef Contest

#59 Welcome to Moldy Manor

The Hunt for the Curious Cheese

#60 The Treasure of Easter Island

#61 Mouse House Hunter

#62 Mouse Overboard!

The Hunt for the Secret Papyrus

#63 The Cheese Experiment

#64 Magical Mission

#65 Bollywood Burglary

The Hunt for the Hundredth Key

#66 Operation: Secret Recipe

#67 The Chocolate Chase

MEET GERONIMO STILTONIX

He is a spacemouse — the Geronimo Stilton of a parallel universe! He is captain of the spaceship *MouseStar 1*. While flying through the cosmos, he visits distant planets and meets crazy aliens. His adventures are out of this world!

#1 Alien Escape

#2 You're Mine, Captain!

#3 Ice Planet Adventure

#4 The Galactic Goal

#5 Rescue Rebellion

#6 The Underwater Planet

#7 Beware! Space Junk!

#8 Away in a Star Sled

#9 Slurp Monster Showdown

#10 Pirate Spacecat Attack

Geronimo Stiltonord

He is a mouseking — the Geronimo Stilton of the ancient far north! He lives with his brawny and brave clan in the village of Mouseborg. From sailing frozen waters to facing fiery dragons, every day is an adventure for the micekings!

#2 The Famouse
Fjord Race

#1 Attack of the
Dragons

#3 Pull the
Dragon's Tooth!

#4 Stay Strong,
Geronimo!

#5 The Mysterious
Message

Don't miss any of these exciting Thea Sisters adventures!

Thea Stilton and the Dragon's Code

Thea Stilton and the Mountain of Fire

Thea Stilton and the Ghost of the Shipwreck

Thea Stilton and the Secret City

Thea Stilton and the Mystery in Paris

Thea Stilton and the Cherry Blossom Adventure

Thea Stilton and the Star Castaways

Thea Stilton: Big Trouble in the Big Apple

Thea Stilton and the Ice Treasure

Thea Stilton and the Secret of the Old Castle

Thea Stilton and the Blue Scarab Hunt

Thea Stilton and the Prince's Emerald

Thea Stilton and the Mystery on the Orient Express

Thea Stilton and the Dancing Shadows

Thea Stilton and the Legend of the Fire Flowers

Thea Stilton and the Spanish Dance Mission

Thea Stilton and the Journey to the Lion's Den

**Thea Stilton and the
Great Tulip Heist**

**Thea Stilton and the
Chocolate Sabotage**

**Thea Stilton and the
Missing Myth**

**Thea Stilton and the
Lost Letters**

**Thea Stilton and the
Tropical Treasure**

**Thea Stilton and the
Hollywood Hoax**

**Thea Stilton and the
Madagascar Madness**

**Thea Stilton and the
Frozen Fiasco**

**Thea Stilton and the
Venice Masquerade**

And check out my fabumouse special editions!

**THEA STILTON:
THE JOURNEY
TO ATLANTIS**

**THEA STILTON:
THE SECRET OF
THE FAIRIES**

**THEA STILTON:
THE SECRET OF
THE SNOW**

**THEA STILTON:
THE CLOUD
CASTLE**

**THEA STILTON:
THE TREASURE
OF THE SEA**

**THEA STILTON:
THE LAND OF
FLOWERS**

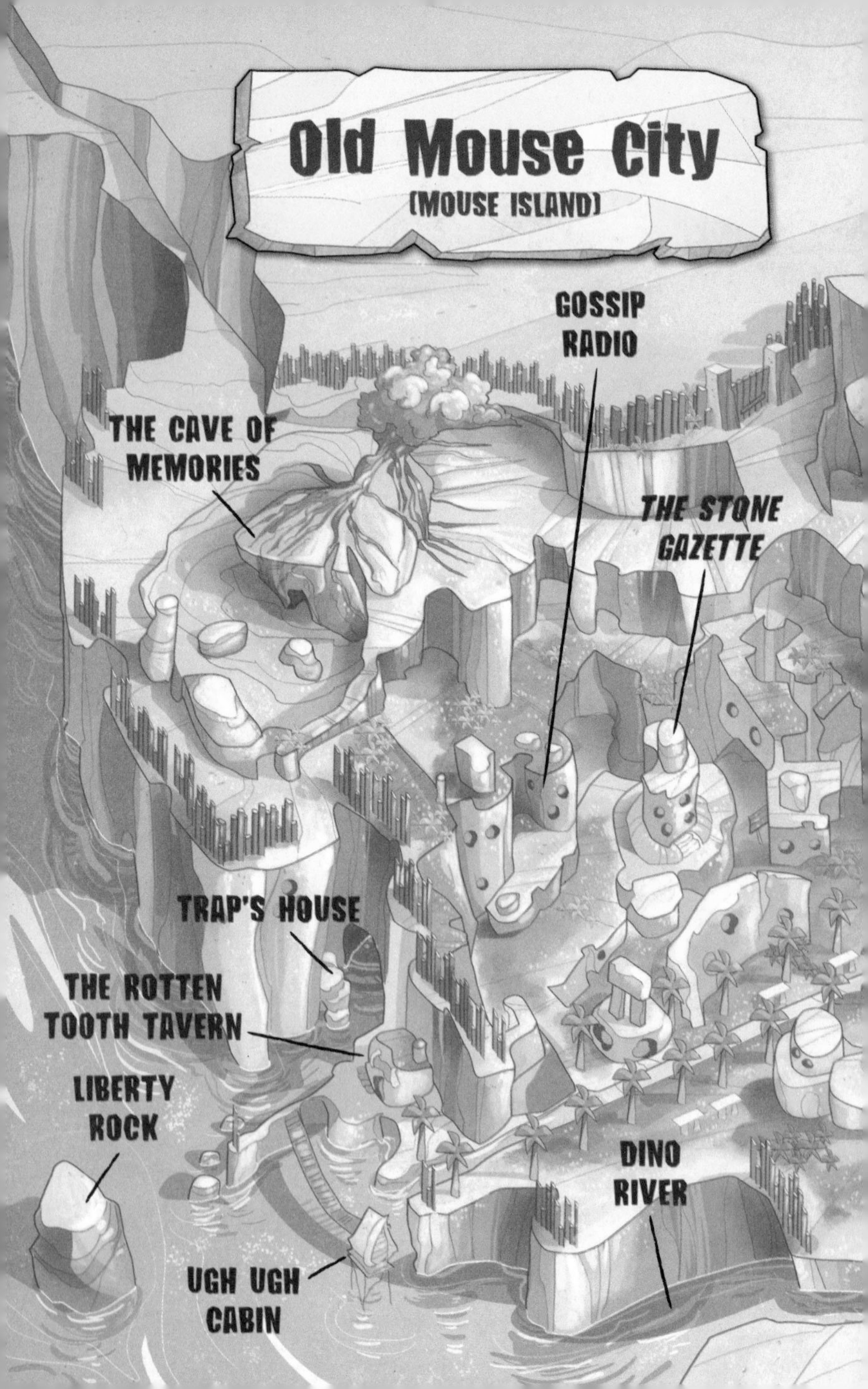

Old Mouse City
(MOUSE ISLAND)

GOSSIP RADIO

THE CAVE OF MEMORIES

THE STONE GAZETTE

TRAP'S HOUSE

THE ROTTEN TOOTH TAVERN

LIBERTY ROCK

DINO RIVER

UGH UGH CABIN

CHEDDAR VOLCANO

SINGING ROCK SQUARE

TYMOUSE HOUSE

HOSPITAL

FLIGHTPORT

SUBWAYSAURUS STATION

THEA'S HOUSE

GRANDMA RATROCK'S HOUSE

GERONIMO'S HOUSE

THE SHAMAN'S GROTTO

DEAR MOUSE FRIENDS,
THANKS FOR READING,
AND GOOD-BYE UNTIL
THE NEXT BOOK!